RAPUNZEL

by the
Brothers Grimm

Illustrated by
Bert Dodson

Troll Associates

Troll Associates, Mahwah, N.J.

Library of Congress Catalog Card Number: 78-18066
ISBN 0-89375-135-9

There once was a man and wife who had wished for a child for a long time. At last it looked as if their wish might come true.

At the back of their house was a window from which the wife could look down on a lovely garden. All around the garden was a high wall. But even if there had been no wall, no one would dare go into the garden, for it belonged to a wicked witch!

One day, the man's wife was looking down from her window, and she happened to see some rampion leaves growing in the garden. Now, she knew how delicious they would taste in a salad, and longed to have some. As

each day passed, she wanted them more and more. Soon, she began to look pale and sick. Her husband asked what was wrong, and she replied, "Alas! I must have some rampion, or I shall die!"

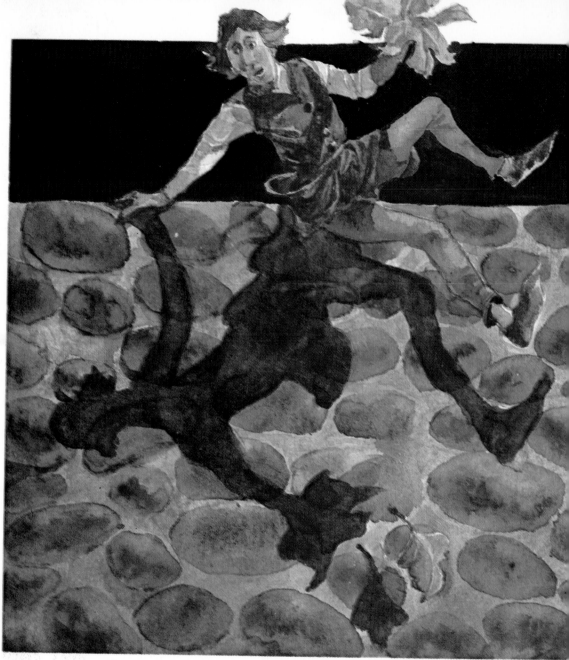

So the husband made up his mind to fetch some. He waited until evening, and then he climbed over the garden wall. In a few moments, he was back, clutching a handful of rampion.

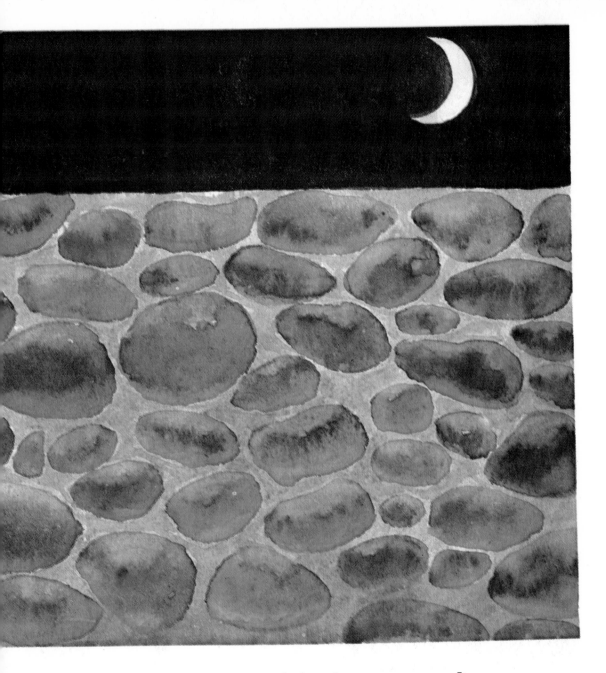

His wife made a salad and ate it at once. It was delicious! In fact, it tasted so good that now she wanted even more rampion!

The next night, the husband crept back over the wall. But just as he was leaving, the witch saw him. "How dare you steal my rampion!" she cried.

"Please," begged the man, "don't hurt me! I only did it for my wife, who thinks she will die without it."

When the witch heard this, she replied, "If that be true, then you may take all the rampion you want. But you must give me something of yours in return. When

your child is born, you must let me have it. I will care for
the child, and treat it just as if it were my very own." The
man was so frightened that he agreed, and quickly fled
from the garden.

Before long, his wife gave birth to a baby girl. When the witch came to take the child away, the woman cried and the man begged and pleaded, but it was no use. The witch took the child and named her Rapunzel.

By the time she grew up, Rapunzel was very beautiful. Her golden hair was the longest and loveliest in all the land. But the witch wanted no one to see Rapunzel's beauty. So she took her into the woods and locked her in a high tower that had no stairs, no doorway, and only one window.

Every day, when the witch came to the tower, she would call out, "Rapunzel, Rapunzel, let down your hair." When Rapunzel heard these words, she would let her long hair hang out the window. Then the witch could climb up, for Rapunzel's hair reached all the way to the ground.

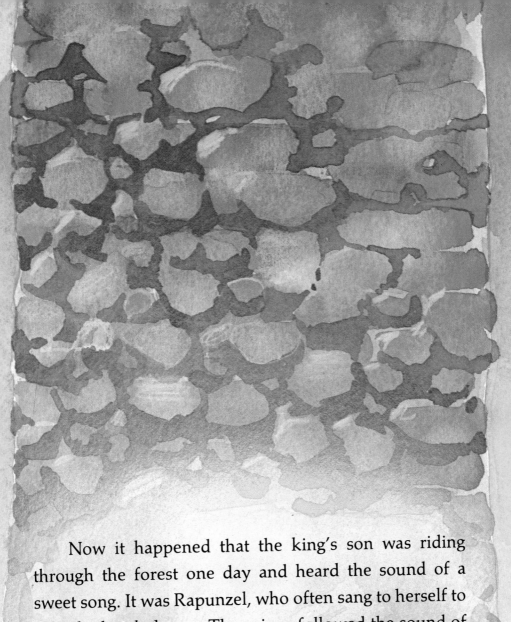

Now it happened that the king's son was riding through the forest one day and heard the sound of a sweet song. It was Rapunzel, who often sang to herself to pass the lonely hours. The prince followed the sound of her voice until he came upon the tower. But since there was no doorway and no staircase, he could not get in, no matter how he tried. Day after day, he returned to the tower to listen to Rapunzel's sweet songs. And soon he began to fall in love with her.

One day, as the prince stood behind a tree, listening
to Rapunzel's songs, the witch appeared. She went to the
bottom of the tower and called, "Rapunzel, Rapunzel, let
down your hair." And then she began climbing up the
long golden hair.

"So that is the way to get into the tower," thought the prince.

The next morning, he went to the tower and called, "Rapunzel, Rapunzel, let down your hair." At once, Rapunzel's hair came tumbling down, and the prince climbed up.

When Rapunzel saw the prince, she was very frightened. She had never seen a man before. But the prince spoke softly to her, and told her of his love. Soon she was no longer afraid. And when the prince asked her to marry him, she agreed.

Then she asked the prince to bring her a piece of silk each time he came to visit her in the tower. "I will twist the silk into a ladder," she said. "When the ladder is long enough, I will climb down from this tower, and we will go away together."

The prince came to see Rapunzel every evening.
Since the witch came only during the day, she didn't
know that Rapunzel had another visitor. And she may
never have known, if Rapunzel hadn't accidentally let the
secret out. But one day, as the witch climbed up to the

window, Rapunzel said, "I wish you could climb up as
fast as the prince ... "

The witch was furious! "So the prince comes to see
you, does he?" she cried. In a rage, she cut off Rapunzel's
hair, which tumbled to the floor in a heap. Then she tied
the hair to the window latch, and took Rapunzel to a
lonely forest far away. She left her there, alone and
miserable.

Then the witch returned to the tower. She climbed
to the top, and pulled Rapunzel's long hair up after her.
When the prince called from below, "Rapunzel, Rapunzel, let down your hair," the witch lowered the long hair

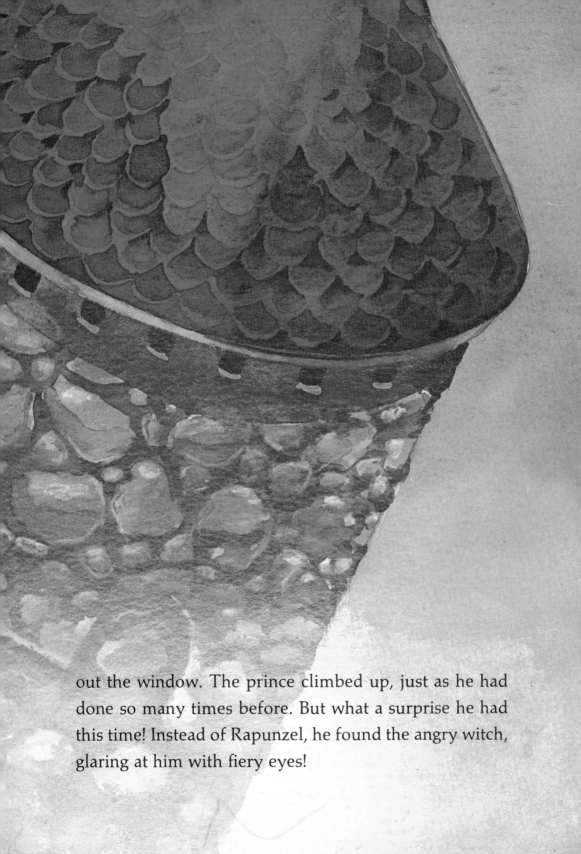

out the window. The prince climbed up, just as he had done so many times before. But what a surprise he had this time! Instead of Rapunzel, he found the angry witch, glaring at him with fiery eyes!

"Aha!" she cried. "You have come for your little bird, but the cat has taken her from the nest. You will never hear her sweet song again!"

The prince was so terrified that he leaped out the window. He landed in a bush of thorns, which scratched his eyes and blinded him.

And so, for many years, the prince wandered blindly through the forest. He was never hungry, for there were roots and berries to eat, but he longed to hear the sweet voice of Rapunzel again. Then one day he

heard a beautiful song drifting through the forest. He
followed the sound, knowing that only one person could
sing so sweetly. It was Rapunzel.

When at last they found each other, tears of joy ran down their cheeks. As Rapunzel wept, two of her tears fell on the prince's eyes and made them well again.

Then the prince led Rapunzel to his kingdom, where they lived happily ever after.